Dear Deer

Dear Deer

A Book of Homophones

GENE BARRETTA

SQUARE
FISH

HENRY HOLT AND COMPANY
NEW YORK

A NOTE TO THE READER

Homophones are words that sound the same but are spelled differently and have different meanings, such as *moose* (the animal) and *mousse* (the dessert). *Homonyms* are words that sound the same and are spelled the same but have different meanings, such as *bowl* (a round dish) and *bowl* (the sport).

SQUARE
FISH

An Imprint of Macmillan

DEAR DEER. Copyright © 2007 by Gene Barretta. All rights reserved.
Printed in China by South China Printing Co. Ltd., Dongguan City, Guangdong Province.
For information, address Square Fish, 175 Fifth Avenue, New York, NY 10010.

Square Fish and the Square Fish logo are trademarks of Macmillan and are used by Henry Holt and Company under license from Macmillan.

Library of Congress Cataloging-in-Publication Data
Barretta, Gene.
Dear deer: a book of homophones / Gene Barretta.
p.   cm.
Summary: When clever Aunt Ant moves to the zoo, she describes the quirky animal behavior she observes by speaking in homophones, from the moose who loved mousse to the fox who blew blue bubbles.
ISBN 978-0-312-62899-4
[1. Homonyms—Fiction. 2. Zoo animals—Fiction.] I. Title. II. Title: Book of homophones.
PZ7.B275366Dea 2007   [E]—dc22   2006031369

Originally published in the United States by Henry Holt and Company
First Square Fish Edition: August 2010

Square Fish logo designed by Filomena Tuosto
Book designed by Laurent Linn
www.mackids.com
10 9 8 7 6

The artist used watercolor on Arches hot-press paper to create the illustrations for this book.

AR: 2.1 / F&P: N / LEXILE: AD530L

For my Deerest Leslie (I'm still fawning)

and all my special Ants: Jane, Kathy, Elaine,

Caroline, Dot, Dee, Sandi, Norma, Josie

—Love, Gene

DEAR DEER,
I now live at the zoo. Wait until you **HEAR** what goes on over **HERE.**

Love,

AUNT ANT

The **MOOSE** loves **MOUSSE**.

He **ATE EIGHT** bowls.

Have **YOU** seen the **EWE?**

She's been in a **DAZE** for **DAYS.**

That's **HIM**, the **HORSE** who is

HOARSE from humming a **HYMN**.

It's quite a **FEAT** when the bat hangs from his **FEET**.

The monkey will tell you a **TALE** as he hangs from his **TAIL**.

The **DOE KNEADED** the **DOUGH,**

because she **NEEDED** the dough.

The **TOAD** was **TOWED**

to the top of the seesaw,

so he could **SEE** the **SEA**.

The **WHALE** was **ALLOWED**

to **WAIL ALOUD**.

The **BEAR** had to **PAUSE**

to **BARE** his big **PAWS**.

HEY, the elephant **THREW** a pail

THROUGH the big bale of **HAY**!

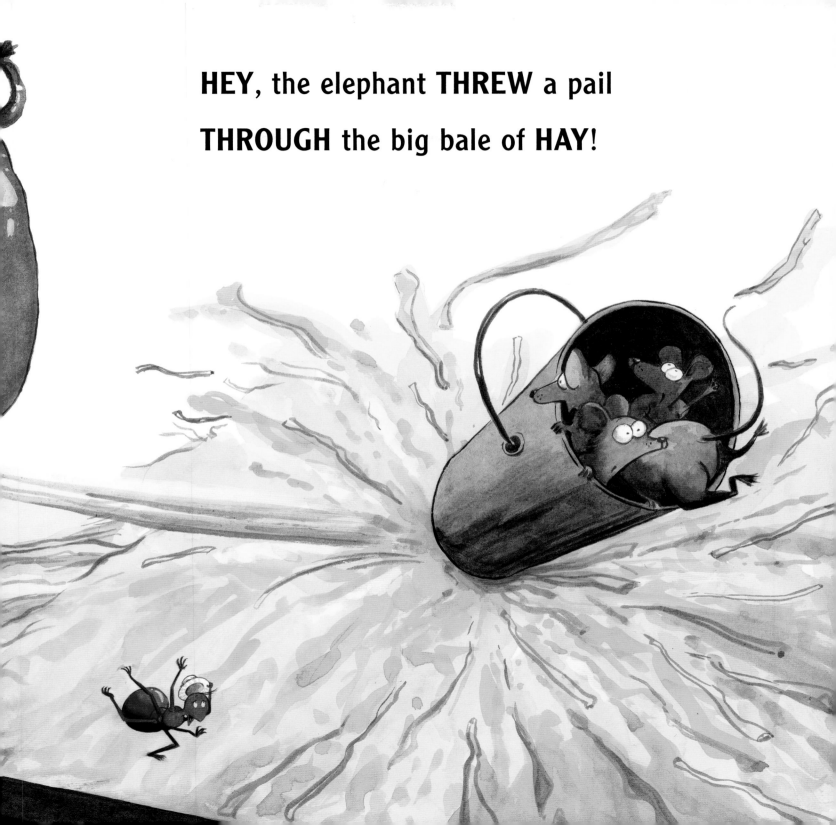

Have you **READ** about the **RED** fox

who **BLEW BLUE** bubbles?

The giraffe's long neck
lets him CHOOSE
what he CHEWS.

The cows in the **HERD**
were in a good **MOOD**.
I HEARD them as they
MOOED in harmony.

The bee **FLEW** away from the flea with the **FLU**. And the **BEE** can **BE** sure that if he had the flu the **FLEA** would **FLEE**, too.

There is no **NEWS** about the **GNUS**.

They keep to themselves.